SNAKE ATTACK

A crack of yellow shone from beneath the bathroom door, but there was no light on in their bedroom. Charlie hesitated, then got out his flashlight instead of turning on the overhead light. Grinning, he set down the bucket, pulled back the covers on John's cot, and switched on his flash.

All he could do was gulp.

The black snake was as thick around as his flashlight and easily five feet long — counting coils. In the wavering light it raised its narrow head and flicked its tongue at him warningly.

Charlie's mouth opened in a soundless scream. . . .

THE
JOKE
WAR

GENE INYART NAMOVICZ

A MINSTREL® BOOK

PUBLISHED BY POCKET BOOKS

New York   London   Toronto   Sydney   Tokyo

A Minstrel Book published by
POCKET BOOKS, a division of Simon & Schuster Inc.
1230 Avenue of the Americas, New York, N.Y. 10020

*This book is dedicated to
Susan, Catherine, Matt, and Daniel Namovicz
with love, respect, and admiration*

THE
JOKE
WAR

Chapter One

Charlie had to be ready as soon as he stepped off the train—or the trick wouldn't work. Because John was quicker than he was. Quicker and smarter.

But maybe not this time.

"Kingston!" called the conductor as he passed Charlie's seat. "Next stop, Kingston!"

When the heavy door wheezed shut, Charlie looked across the aisle. No problem. The man in the black shirt and bright yellow tie was still reading his newspaper. Very carefully, Charlie took the plump rubber glove out of his duffle bag. It jiggled in his hands, alive like a little animal. Smooth and warm. Tight as a drum. The rubber band hadn't snapped and the tape over the pinhole hadn't slipped.

"All ri-ight!" he whispered, satisfied. If this thing

worked, John would see that he was fun to have around—that he wasn't a kid anymore. Then maybe he wouldn't go off with Pete all the time.

But Charlie had to be on guard. When John got talking, it was hard to do anything but listen. When he smiled at people he hypnotized them the way snakes did birds. Rosie was immune, but not Charlie. Every summer he was a dumb bird again, waiting to be swallowed.

"Kingston!" bellowed the conductor from the end of the car.

The man across the aisle swung down his suitcase from the overhead rack. "Who's the victim?" he asked in a hoarse whisper, giving Charlie a knowing smile.

"My cousin," Charlie said unwillingly.

"What've you got in the rubber glove? Ketchup?"

"Grape Kool-Aid."

"Kool-Aid?" The big man guffawed. "You ever tried this trick before?"

Charlie shook his head, wishing the man would get out of his way. "No."

"Want any help?"

"No!" said Charlie again. Couldn't he see there wasn't time?

The big man shrugged and lumbered toward the door.

Gingerly, Charlie draped his jacket over the rubber glove, picked up his duffle bag, and got to his feet. He had to stay calm now. Had to be relaxed but ready for anything. Last year, a split second after he got off the train, John had slipped a live goldfish down his neck. And two years ago he had yelled "Catch!" and tossed Charlie a raw egg.

With a series of bumps and screeches the train jerked to a stop. Charlie grabbed hold of a seatback to keep from lurching into the nosy man and tried to see out the window. What if they were late? What if he had to stand there on the platform with the stupid glove sticking out from under his jacket?

"Are you sure you don't want any help, kid?"

The guy wouldn't let it go. When he turned, his face hung over Charlie's like a balloon. The boy shook his head and backed up.

"You're on my foot," said the woman behind him.

Charlie stepped forward hastily. Why didn't the porter open the door? he wondered. Mashed in here like a slice of salami, he couldn't see through the window—couldn't see what John was doing out there.

The nosy man turned around again, his eyes shiny with curiosity. "Say, I've done that trick a few times. Can I give you a word of advice?"

"No," said Charlie for what he hoped was the last time. The important thing was not to let the man rattle him. All he had to do was connect with John before John got to him.

"ALLIE!" The lady behind him waved wildly to someone down on the platform. "Allie, I do believe you've put on ten pounds!" she shouted—and nudged Charlie out of the car with her suitcase. Not until then did he realize that the door was open and the platform steps in place. The man in the black shirt and yellow tie stepped off the train, and Charlie jumped down after him.

Right away he saw them—Aunt Edie, slim and tan as always—Rosie, who was a year younger than he was and nicer than a sister—and John. Tall, handsome, sure of himself, not-quite-twelve John.

Timing. That was what mattered now. Charlie felt the sweat break out on his forehead, felt the plump rubber glove turn slippery in his anxious hands. He had to get the timing just right.

"Hello, Charlie!" said Aunt Edie.

"Hi, Charlie!" said Rosie, grinning.

Then John smiled at him—smiled a smile of unholy glee and lifted his eyebrows teasingly.

Charlie panicked. He fumbled with the masking tape on the forefinger of the loaded rubber glove—the finger he'd made the pinhole in. But before he could pull the tape off, John reached out and squeezed the glove as if he were shaking someone's hand. Squeezed it hard enough to push off the rubber band. Hard enough so that the grape Kool-Aid shot out the back of the glove—right smack at Charlie.

"Charlie!" gasped Aunt Edie, horrified. "What have you done to yourself?"

Chapter Two

Purple Kool-Aid trickled down Charlie's white shirt onto his tan slacks. He could feel the wet stickiness spreading, but he didn't want to look at it. He didn't want to look at John either because he was dancing around the platform like a wild man, screaming with laughter and pointing his finger at Charlie.

"You look like—like—half a jelly sandwich," he managed to choke out.

"Stop making fun of him!" Rosie said angrily.

"I—can't—help—it." John laughed so hard he cried. "I really can't!" he gasped, patting Charlie on the shoulder. He wiped his eyes and motioned toward his mother. "Anyway, it's all her fault."

"That's not true!" said Aunt Edie.

"It is, too! You're the one who made me promise not to play a trick on Charlie when he got off the train." John turned to Rosie. "And you—you were dead wrong. He does so like practical jokes, or he wouldn't have tried to pull one on me!"

Charlie's face grew warm with pleasure. So what if the trick hadn't worked? Just trying had been enough to make John notice him.

"That was a good one, Charlie, but you've got to move faster." John picked up the limp rubber glove and held it at arm's length as if it smelled bad. "Once I caught sight of this fellow, I knew what was coming. What you should have done—"

"Enough!" said Aunt Edie. She opened the door of the blue station wagon and slid in behind the wheel. "He's been on the train since six o'clock this morning—and you've just shot purple ink on his best clothes. Honestly, John! I wish you'd learn. Some things are simply not funny."

"Hey, he did it himself," John said happily. "Don't you get all steamed up about it, Mom. Charlie isn't."

"Enough, I said. Get in! Let's go home."

"All right, all right." John pushed Charlie and the duffle bag into the middle seat, and climbed in himself. "What you should have done is put some of that grape stuff in a balloon and wrap the balloon in tissue paper. Then you could have burst it with a pin after you handed it to me."

6

"I was only trying to—"

"Hey, don't worry about it. With Pete off at tennis camp it's been dull as dishwater here. We can work on it together until we get it right."

Charlie nodded, feeling pretty good. If Pete wasn't here, John would have to spend more time with Rosie and him. It was a good thing he'd brought his new book and the kite stuff. John hadn't sounded interested when they talked on the phone, but that was because he didn't know all the things you could do with kites.

"Did you have a good trip, Charlie?"

"Yes," he said, smiling at Aunt Edie's face in the rear view mirror. Because he didn't see her very often, he was always surprised at how much she looked like his mother—and even sounded like her. "Mom said she hopes you finish your thesis soon."

John snorted. "*She* hopes so, does she? How do you think the rest of us feel? Even the mice are starving. I went in the kitchen yesterday morning and there were footprints in the butter. Last night a bunch of them climbed up on the table and gnawed holes in all the green peaches. Even when Mom remembers to buy groceries, we're the ones who have to cook."

"*Who* has to cook?" asked Aunt Edie, raising an eyebrow.

"I have to cook!" said Rosie.

"Hey, I only missed a couple of times," John said.

"Anyway, now there'll be three of us taking turns. Isn't that right, Charlie?" he said, grinning and holding out his right hand.

Charlie remembered that gesture from three summers ago—knew beyond the shadow of a doubt that John had an electric buzzer in the palm of his hand. Any idiot who touched him would get his hair curled. Only this time Charlie wasn't going to be the idiot.

John's eyes glowed. "Isn't that right?" he said again, leaning closer.

"Right," said Charlie, keeping his arms close to his sides.

"Right on!" said John, and tapped him lightly on the chest.

"YE-OWW!" yelped Charlie.

"MOM!" Rosie shouted. "John broke his promise. You told him not to do anything to Charlie, and he just gave him a shock."

"Hey, come on, Rosie! It was only supposed to be a little buzz. I just forgot he was wet." Looking anxious, John dabbed at the stain on Charlie's shirt. "There you go, fellow. Just relax now. You're going to be all right, aren't you?"

"Ulp," went Charlie, still trying to get his breath.

"Sorry there was so much kick to it," John said. He brightened. "Tell you what. I'll make it up to you. Why don't you try another joke on me? I promise I won't get mad the way some people do." He looked meaningfully at Rosie. "Nobody else in this family likes practical jokes."

"For once you're right about something," said Rosie.

"Well, relax. I won't bother you anymore now." John turned to Charlie. "You can do anything at all! The wilder the better." He smiled a smile that lit up his whole face. "Hey! What do you say we make it a contest? See which of us can pull the wildest trick on the other? Come on! Have a stick of gum to seal the bargain?"

"Don't!" warned Rosie, twisting around in her seat. "Touch that gum and you'll lose a finger!"

Smirking at Rosie, John shoved a stick of gum in his mouth and offered the pack to Charlie.

Warily, Charlie took a piece. When nothing snapped at him, he unwrapped it and started chewing. "This contest," he began, hesitant. "What sort of thing did you have in mind?"

"You pull a trick on me, then I play one on you. Just a game to make the time pass. Hey? Remember the year we ran those little tin boats back and forth across the tide pool up at the point and pretended it was the Spanish Armada? That was fun, wasn't it?"

Six-inch-long boats powered by little candles—but John had made fragile shell sails for each one. Charlie smiled, remembering how the three of them had stretched out on their stomachs to watch the tiny fleet putt-putt back and forth across the shining pool.

"The birthday candle boats!" said Rosie. "I remember those!" she said, turning excitedly. Then her eyes widened. "Yu-uck, Charlie! Your teeth have turned black!" She shook her mother's arm. "MOM! John did it again. He played another trick on Charlie!"

Charlie gagged.

"Don't do that, Charlie!" Aunt Edie yelled, slamming on the brakes. "Don't touch me when I'm driving, Rosie!" she said in a steely voice. Then, leaning her forehead against the steering wheel, she added softly. "John, I want you to do something for me."

"What?"

"Stop it!"

"Don't worry, Mom," Rosie said soothingly. "We're home now. Come on! Get out of the car. If the tide's in, we can go for a nice cool swim."

"Don't worry, Mom," John said, patting her on the shoulder. "Trust me! Charlie and I are going to have a blast this summer."

Chapter Three

Charlie was the first one out of the car when Aunt Edie pulled into her parking place between the apple tree and the poison ivy. When she unlocked the back door, he was first into the house.

The kitchen was the same. It smelled of fresh peaches ripening in the window. Charlie sniffed, then, conscious of someone on his heels, he swung around.

"Don't worry. It's me," said Rosie.

"Where's John?"

"He left to go with Pete's brother on his boat. Pete always helped Ed check the lobster pots and John's taking his place while he's away."

"Oh?" said Charlie. With a lighter step, he moved catlike through the cottage, making it his own again.

The dining room, too, was the way he remembered—all afternoon sunlight. One of Aunt Edie's droopy wildflower arrangements stood in the middle of the bare oak table. Through the dusty window he could see a row of bright-spinnakered sailboats floating up the bay.

"Be careful of John this summer," Rosie said matter-of-factly. She picked up the binoculars from the corner cupboard and trained them on the lead boats.

Charlie stiffened. "How come?"

Rosie gave him a disgusted look. "He's like a toaster about to pop up. Can't you tell? Ever since Pete left he's driven us bonkers playing tricks. That's why Mom said he couldn't pull anything on you at the station."

"He's always been like that." Charlie unhooked the screen door and stepped out on the porch. The sun was bright on the blue water and he stood there in a happy daze, staring out at the bay.

Rosie followed him outside. "He's always been a pain, but now he's lethal. It's gotten out of hand, Charlie. You'd better do what I do and ignore him."

"*Ignore* him?"

"Sure! Just for five or ten years. He'll probably be all right when he grows up."

Behind them, the screen door creaked and both of them jumped.

"Poor Charlie," Aunt Edie said, and sank into the lounger. "Why don't you change into your bathing suit and give me those clothes? What is that purple stuff?"

"Grape Kool-Aid," Charlie said, shamefaced.

Aunt Edie groaned. "I make no promises about the shirt, but the black will come off your teeth with a little baking soda."

"Mom," said Rosie suddenly. "You heard John trying to con Charlie into a wild tricks contest, didn't you?"

"I try not to listen to any of you in the car. It keeps me from driving up telephone poles."

"Come on, Mom! You heard him. I know you did. Tell Charlie not to do it—not to mess with John at all."

Aunt Edie gave her a level stare. "I seem to remember that Charlie started it this time." She gave him an apologetic smile. "Now why don't the two of you put on your suits so we can have a swim before supper?" Charlie smiled back at her and she shuddered. "And, for heaven sakes, Rosie! Find him the baking soda."

"Is she mad at us?" Charlie asked, as he followed Rosie up the narrow stairway with his duffle bag.

"Actually, she's mad at John—but she's trying to be fair. She's mad at Dad, too, because he can only be here weekends." Rosie pulled back the door curtain. "You're in with John again. He's got the cot closest to the window—as always."

"That's all right." He liked having his bed against

Rosie's wall. That way they could whisper to one another through the knothole after John fell asleep. Content, Charlie dropped his bag beside the bed and walked over to the window.

Sometimes the bridge was only partly there—half smudged out by the fog—but today it was a sharp silver arc across the bright water. He smiled and sank into the wicker chair.

Too late, Rosie cried out.

"Whoa!" went Charlie as he toppled over backwards and cracked his head on the floor.

"Sorry about that," Rosie said, offering him a hand up. She turned the chair upside down. "There! I knew it!" she said. "John pulled a switch on you. This is the broken one from the storage closet. He propped it up with a piece of cardboard."

Charlie touched the back of his head carefully. "Where's the baking soda?"

"There's a box in our bathroom." Rosie hesitated. "Is that what you're going to do? Clean your teeth?"

"And change. Your mother said we could go swimming."

"Without checking out the rest of the room?" Rosie's face paled behind her freckles. "Good grief! Do you think he stopped with the chair?"

"I didn't ask to have a contest."

"Think for a minute, Charlie." Rosie stood in the middle of the room and turned in a slow circle, studying the walls, the window, the ceiling. "He hasn't been in here since we met your train."

"You mean, he'd already planted a bunch of booby traps?"

"All he promised was not to do anything when you got off the train."

"Oh, well," Charlie said, managing a grin. He'd wanted John to pay attention to him, hadn't he? "What's the big deal? A buzz every now and then. A fly in the soup. Hey, I can handle it."

"Hey?" mocked Rosie. She kicked at the fiber carpet under Charlie's bed—then jumped back when a mousetrap snapped shut. "Hah!"

Charlie took a deep breath. "About how many more things do you think there'll be?" he said, pushing the mousetrap aside with the toe of his shoe.

"Well, let's see. He knew you'd go over to the window. What else would he do?" Rosie considered. "I think there'll be something in the drawers, something in the bathroom, and maybe something in the bed itself."

Short sheets probably. No, that was too simple. But wait—that's what John would figure he'd think. With a sigh, Charlie stripped the bed and remade it. He took the pillow out of the case, shook it, and put that back, too. Nothing again.

Rosie watched sympathetically. "Maybe I was wrong. Tell you what—I'll help you check the dresser." She crossed the room warily. "Careful now," she murmured. Leaning way over to the side, she pulled the top drawer open an inch at a time. Then, cautiously, she looked inside.

Charlie looked in, too. A dusty, empty drawer. He closed it and began to tug at the next one.

"Stay to one side!"

Feeling foolish, Charlie leaned a little bit to the right. Enough for the ripe tomato that shot out of the drawer to miss hitting him full in the face. Not enough to keep his left cheek from being smeared with bright red pulp.

"Oh, boy!" said Rosie, rueful. "Sorry about that, too." She hitched up her shorts and looked at him thoughtfully. "You know, you're getting pretty grubby looking. Maybe we ought to go swimming?"

"How did he do it?" Charlie asked very calmly, wiping the tomato seeds off his mouth. Pale juice trickled down his neck and blended with the purple on his shirt.

"It's an old jack-in-the-box. John uses those a lot. He fastens something to the spring, then sets it so the release is triggered when you open the door or drawer." She dropped the little square box into the wastebasket. "Want me to scrape you off?"

"No, thanks." Charlie got out his toothbrush and headed for the bathroom.

"Watch out in there!" Rosie called after him.

"Right," he said. He put the hook on the door and looked around. How could you booby-trap a bathroom? Forget the tub because he didn't need it. He was careful flushing the toilet, but it didn't overflow—careful turning on the faucets, but water didn't spurt out at him. The mirror over the sink looked innocent and normal, but the face in it wasn't. Pinkish tomato pulp decorated one side of his face—and his teeth were black.

Black and rotten looking.

"Yuck!" He ripped off his stained shirt and balled it up. Then he worked up a good suds with his hands and washed off the tomato stuff.

That was better. Lots better, he decided, rubbing his face dry on the big white towel.

What he had to do was concentrate—pay attention to one thing at a time and not get rattled. Grimly, he dumped baking soda in his hand, dug into it with his wet toothbrush, and started brushing. He didn't even look in the mirror until he had scrubbed his teeth up and down and sideways.

Then he choked. His teeth were white enough for a toothpaste commercial. But his face—now his face was green.

Dumb! Dumb! Dumb! He'd remembered not to use the washcloth, but forgotten about the towel. Stupid towel! He hurled it to the floor, splashed water on his face, and rubbed the bar of soap over his cheeks again, working up a thick lather. A great lather, he decided, admiring it in the mirror. Like his father got when he was shaving. Except—except that this lather had a sort of greenish cast. Almost as if—

No! It couldn't be.

But it was. He scraped off the foam and stared into the mirror. Yuck! Now his face was even greener. It had to be the soap—that innocent looking bar of white soap.

"Everything all right?" Rosie asked from outside the door.

"What could be wrong?" Charlie said bitterly.

"Want me to wait for you?"

"No, go on," he said, smearing baking soda on his face. He rubbed it in, added a glob of damp scouring powder and scrubbed harder. Pretty soon the face in the mirror changed from green to red.

Charlie groaned. No skin left, but at least he looked like a human being again. With a sigh of relief, he went back to his room and sat down on the bed—which gave way under him with a soft, smacking thump.

There wasn't much noise because there wasn't anything much left to clatter. John had simply removed the bed slats.

Chapter Four

Ten minutes later, Charlie ran out the door with his smallest box kite and jumped off the sea wall onto the beach. Both the bat kite and the big blue fish had looked tempting when he sorted through his stuff, but he knew the box was steadier. Most times he could get it up pretty fast, too. Best to have it airborne when he ran into the others so that he could offer John a live string. Grinning, he licked a finger and tested the wind.

Offshore a fishing boat pulled up anchor and started its motor. Charlie shaded his eyes from the glare. Could that be Pete's brother's boat? Nope. Only men on board—no sign of a tall slim boy in tennis shorts. No telling where John was now. Better get going.

Back to the wind, he held the kite high in his left hand and began slowly unwinding its string as he walked, trying not to trip on a rock. Open fields were easier. Here he was apt to fall on his face. But the wind was strong and the wind had caught the box kite. The string pulled and tugged in his grasp and he unreeled faster and faster, running now, laughing as the bright yellow square climbed higher and higher into the blue—and then the string snapped.

A gull screamed. Charlie watched the yellow dot in the sky until it disappeared over Newport, then he turned his burning face to the breeze. The tide had turned, leaving a rim of bright green eel grass on the shore, and the air had a fresh and fishy smell. It was hard to feel bad about a kite set free, he thought, smiling.

"Hey, Charlie?"

He swung around. John—shirtless and tanned—leapt off the sea wall and loped toward him.

"Hey, Charlie? Want to go up to the point? Some guy's built a big house up there and a pier that goes way out into the bay. He's even got a boat we can dive off of—that is, if you want to try it?"

Did he want to try it? That was one of the things he liked about John. He had a good idea every ten minutes. Of course, sometimes you were sorry if you went along with them.

"Come on, Charlie! I've been waiting for you to get here so we could have some fun. All Rosie cares about is collecting specimens for her dumb aquariums."

John really seemed to mean it. For a moment Charlie's heart lifted, then he caught himself. What if this was another practical joke? "Are you sure it's all right to swim there?" Other summers Aunt Edie had made them go swimming right here in front of the cottage.

John shrugged out of his shorts so that he was in swim trunks, too. "Sure! We don't need to go on the yacht. We'll dive off the rope ladder."

Charlie studied the horizon. If there was a house up at the point, it was hidden by the scrub trees that grew back of the beach. But he could see a new dock and, moored at the end of it, a big white yacht.

"Come on!" John yelled, and started running.

Charlie took off after him, stumbling along the rocky beach.

"Hurry up, slowpoke!"

John was way ahead and widening the distance between them—but Charlie was still stiff from the train. Not limbered up yet. John was almost to the point—almost even with the white yacht—already wading into the water.

The water? Panting, Charlie ran on doggedly, casting a longing look at the choppy blue waves. The tide had just turned, so it was still deep enough to swim. And, swimming, he could catch up with John. Without breaking stride, he splashed into the bay, flinching as the icy water seeped into his sneakers. Aunt Edie made them wear shoes so they wouldn't cut their feet on the barnacles, and he was glad of it. Better than stepping on squishy things barefooted.

"Hurry!" John shouted.

Charlie was in the eel grass now. Leafy runners wound themselves around his legs, tickling him— making him think of jellyfish and octopuses and real eels. And it was cold. He was in up to his thighs and he was numb.

John surprised him by waiting until he caught up. "Race you out to the boat?" he said with a grin.

"You're on!" cried Charlie, gritting his teeth. "Go!"

Together they dove into the waist-deep water. Charlie felt it rush up his nose, fill his ears. He tasted the salt of it in his mouth. "YE-OWW!" he yelled with joy. He started swimming hard—just a crawl at first, then, when he noticed that John was ahead of him and going strong—a slower, steadier breaststroke, his head bobbing up and down like a seal in the rocking water.

"Still coming?" John called over his shoulder.

Charlie saved his breath and kept on swimming. John was as good as ever, but Charlie had practiced all winter. Now he had a chance to win. The white yacht was suddenly close, looming above the waterline. Her name, painted in gold, was *The Gangi Grocer*.

"Still coming?" spluttered John, only a length in the lead now.

Charlie flipped over and shot ahead with his back-

22

stroke. Ten yards later he touched *The Gangi Grocer*'s hull with the flat of his hand, grinning in triumph.

"You've gotten good, haven't you?" John called ruefully as he swam up.

"Better anyway," said Charlie, embarrassed.

John's eyes glinted with sudden laughter. "Tell you what," he said, slapping Charlie on the shoulder. "You're the winner—you take the first dive."

The ladder was slender and slippery, dangling loosely against the side of the yacht so that Charlie couldn't seem to climb up until John steadied it. Even then he kept swinging out of control, losing his grip.

Down below, John was getting impatient. "Move, Charlie!"

"What's going on?" came a bellow from overhead.

Dizzily, Charlie looked straight up. It was the man from the train—the nosy one who'd wanted to give him advice. Only now he wasn't smiling.

"You boys again, is it? I told you what I'd do if you came back."

Charlie saw the bucket upended over his head— saw the stuff sliding out of the bucket. He saw it all, but he didn't understand what was happening until the garbage hit him in the face.

Chapter Five

"That wasn't funny," Charlie said, staggering out of the water. He gave John a black look.

"Honest, Charlie, I didn't plan to do it! When I heard him on the boat, it came to me like a bolt out of the blue. Anyway, you *were* funny, dangling there with your mouth open. I was afraid you'd swallow that stuff."

"JOHN? CHARLIE?" Rosie jumped from rock to rock, running toward them. "JOH-UNNN! Mom says come back near the cottage and swim where she can lifeguard you."

Whistling softly, John leaned over to retie his shoe. "The thing is, no one knows who this guy is, or how come he has such a big yacht. I tried to go on board once myself and he chased me away."

"Why didn't you warn me?"

"Because you never would have climbed up there if you'd known he dumped bilge water on me."

Rosie ran up to them, panting. "What's going on?"

"Ask Charlie. It's my turn to cook supper tonight." John grinned, and took off toward the cottage.

"What's wrong?"

"Nothing." Then Charlie blushed. Feeling even dumber than he'd been feeling, he started off after John.

"Wait! Come look at my aquarium?"

"Later, maybe."

"Now," Rosie urged. "Come on, Charlie! I've got a scallop. Did you know that scallops have blue eyes?"

He stopped in surprise. "I didn't know they had eyes."

"They do. Lots of them. Come on, I'll show you." She ran ahead of him to where the rocky beach smoothed out into a stretch of layered slate, and hauled a washtub full of sea water out of the bushes.

"Look!" she said as he knelt beside her. "I found a three-legged starfish for you. Remember? You wanted to see if they really do grow more legs." Without giving him time to answer, she went on quickly. "And I've got a whole bunch of hermit crabs, and three limpets, and a scallop. Watch, Charlie!" she said eagerly. "I can't take him out of the water or he won't do it, but watch him when I drop this little hermit crab next to him."

Charlie watched. The scallop was fan shaped and symmetrical like the hundred million empty shells he'd picked up on the beach. But then, as the tiny snail-shelled crab drifted down and came to rest beside it, the miracle happened. The top and bottom sections of the scallop parted a fraction of an inch—like the lid of a little box lifting—and he saw a whole row of bright blue eyes staring back at him. Then, plop! The lid slammed shut.

"I don't believe it," he said softly.

Rosie was pleased. "I knew you'd like it," she said. Then she leaned toward him, her eyes glowing. "Do you know what else I finally found?"

"What?"

"Sea anemones!"

Charlie drew a blank. "Show me!"

"I can't." She sounded mad. "You probably couldn't get them into an aquarium even if you wanted to—but they're nicer where they are anyway. Except that I can't take you there."

"Why not? Where are they?"

"Up at the point. About four feet offshore at low tide—under the grouchy man's new pier."

"I don't see why you can't show them to me. After a couple of days, I mean." The man had seemed friendly enough on the train. "He won't throw garbage on us for walking under the pier, will he?"

"No, but he'll yell at us. I can't even walk that way

anymore without being yelled at. He thinks the whole beach is his just because he built that stupid big house." Suddenly she smiled. "Hey, I know what! I could show you some sea anemones at Beavertail. The park ranger showed them to me." She pushed the washtub back into the shade. "Want to see if Mom'll let us go to Beavertail tomorrow?"

Charlie hesitated. "Do you think John would go with us?"

Rosie made a face at him. "I told you to ignore him." Then she relented. "You know he only goes at high tide during a storm when it's really wild."

She was right, of course. John didn't like sifting through the sheltered tide pools and talking to fishermen the way he and Rosie did. John didn't even think it was special just to *be* there at the tip of the island with the wind and the spray smacking you and blowing away your words when you tried to talk to one another.

"Never mind!" said Rosie. She got to her feet. "But be careful."

"What do you mean?"

"Face it! John's not even warmed up yet."

Charlie's finger discovered some eggshell behind his right ear. Furtively, he flicked it away. "I can take care of myself," he said in a firm voice.

"Ro-seee! Char-leee!" Aunt Edie called from the sea wall. "Supper's ready. Come and get it!"

"I like my hot dogs cooked on a stick," Rosie complained.

"Too bad!" said John. "I boiled everything because Mom had put the corn water on for me. Tomorrow you can roast anything you like on a stick."

"Tomorrow Rosie can do pizza," Aunt Edie said absently, without taking her eyes from her murder mystery. "And Tuesday we're having hamburgers." She looked up at Charlie. "Can you cook hamburgers?"

"Sure!" he said, startled. Probably even his cat, Homer, could cook hamburgers.

"Good," said Aunt Edie. "You may have Tuesday. Then back to John on Wednesday—Rosie on Thursday—and you again on Friday, Charlie."

"She cooks on weekends when Dad comes home," Rosie explained to Charlie. "Of course, it would be safer to save John for then. Dad would never let him get away with putting raisins in the chili."

"Hey?" said John piously. "I forgot you hate raisins."

"Don't forget again," said Aunt Edie. "Cook's rules. Please most of the people most of the time." She looked at each of them in turn. "And don't any of you forget—absolutely no funny business when you're cooking. No wasting food. Understand?"

"Absolutely!" said John, one hand over his heart. "No wasting food. Right, Charlie?"

"Right," Charlie said doubtfully. He was starving, but he took time to check out the table. It looked safe enough. Hot dogs on rolls, corn on the cob, and, for dessert, strawberry shortcake. Relieved, he chose an ear of corn from the center of the platter, buttered and salted it, and ate it happily. Definitely not the corn. He helped himself to a second ear, then a third.

"Hey? Nobody's eating the hot dogs. My hot dogs are getting cold!" John wailed.

"People always eat the corn first. But I'd love a hot dog now," his mother said, holding out her plate.

With the tongs, John zapped a hot dog onto a roll and handed it to her. "Rosie?" he asked, grinning.

"I'll pick my own," Rosie said, and forked herself one.

"How about you, Charlie?" asked John—without much hope. "Can I do you one?"

"Why not?"

Eyebrows raised in surprise, John plunked a hot dog on a roll and passed it along, helping himself as well. "Well, it's good to be eating. People say that having to cook spoils your appetite, but I'm hungry enough to eat an old rubber boot."

Charlie squirted a trail of mustard along his hot dog, and bit in.

"Way to go, Charlie!" John cheered as the hot dog shot out of the bun, flew across the dining room, and bounced off Great-aunt Evelyn's black-lacquered writing desk.

Licking the mustard off his chin, Charlie stared at John accusingly. "It was rubber, wasn't it?"

"Plastic, as a matter of fact." John laughed and nudged his mother in the ribs. "Hey, Mom? Look at the expression on Charlie's face."

Aunt Edie stared at Charlie and then slammed down her book. "John, how could you? You promised you wouldn't ruin the food."

"I didn't! All I did was slip him a nice clean plastic hot dog—simmered right along with the others, served piping hot on a fresh roll. No harm done. Right, Charlie?"

Charlie nodded unhappily, and speared himself a real hot dog.

"Well, then," said John, grinning. He poured out four glasses of iced tea and passed them around. "No hard feelings?" he said, clinking glasses with Charlie.

"No hard feelings," Charlie managed.

Rosie shook her head at him in despair. "No hard feelings, yourself, stupid! He's put a bug in your iced tea."

Charlie choked.

"Easy now!" John warned, jerking his head toward his mother, who was caught up again in her mystery novel. "Don't unsettle the natives. That's a nice, clean plastic ice cube with a plastic fly inside. If you like, I'll trade glasses with you."

"No problem," said Charlie, trying to sound casual.

30

"Well, all right then," said John, smiling. "But you're getting way behind, you know. When are you going to play a trick on me?"

When indeed? wondered Charlie. He closed his eyes and drank his iced tea.

Chapter Six

Three hours later he had it sorted out. The question wasn't when he was going to play a trick on John. It was what trick he was going to play. First he had to get an idea.

"Come inside or the mosquitoes will eat you alive!" Aunt Edie called.

"In a minute," said Charlie. He leaned back against the porch post and looked out at the darkening bay. The moon was a balloon—a big orange glob. Across on the Newport shore the lights were coming on like popcorn popping. On the other side of the double screen doors, Aunt Edie sat knitting and reading in a pool of lamplight.

Happy as a clam, she was. All she had to do was

work on her thesis and read murder mysteries, while John fed him rubber hot dogs, or strychnine, or whatever. Charlie sighed. He couldn't just sit here like a bump on a log. He had to come up with something.

"Are you still out there, Charlie?" Rosie called from the dining room.

"Yes." She was sitting at the oak table, playing solitaire.

"Want to play cards?"

"No. Thanks, anyway." Rosie was nice that way, trying to cheer him up in case he was homesick the first night, the way he'd been when he was younger. Charlie stared at the three little boats moving over the dark water. Like waterbugs with lanterns. As soon as the third one reached the river of moonlight, he would go inside and look for John. But what would he do when he found him?

"Rosie?" Aunt Edie said suddenly. "Did you move that bucket of hermit crabs from the porch?"

"No. None of them were different enough to keep. I'll throw them back in the water in the morning."

"Throw them back tonight," said her mother. "Otherwise we'll have standing-room-only skunks serving themselves on the porch."

Charlie stood up and stretched. "I'll do it, Rosie."

"Thanks!"

He took the bucket out to the sea wall. The tide was too low to risk tossing it, so he jumped down to the beach, setting off a wild scrabbling in the pot. Whistling under his breath, he submerged it, and let the frothy black water sweep the crabs away. Then, in the darkness, he felt the bucket jerk in his grasp. What had he caught?

A big, blue crab. Not a hermit. Not a little wisp of a thing living in a cast-off shell, but a blue. Curious, he tilted the container toward the moonlight to get a better look. At least an eight-incher. Charlie looked at it admiringly, and raised the bucket to pitch it back. Would Rosie want it? Probably not. It was big enough to eat everything else in her aquarium and give her a pinch besides.

Pinch?

Charlie righted the bucket while he thought about it. Everything depended on what John was doing right now. Moving as jauntily as he could, he marched up on the porch and into the dining room, where Rosie was still shuffling cards at the table.

"I dumped them in the bay," he said, before she had time to ask. "Where's John?"

"Upstairs bathroom." The bucket made an angry noise and Rosie narrowed her eyes at it. "Sometimes he stays there awhile, but you can't count on it."

"I don't need much time," said Charlie. He walked boldly past Aunt Edie, who was still in the living room, knitting and reading, and ran up the steps. All he had to do was tuck this fellow into John's bed. The crab would do the rest.

A crack of yellow shone from beneath the bathroom door, but there was no light on in their bedroom. Charlie hesitated, then got out his flashlight instead of turning on the overhead light. This way John wouldn't even know he'd been in the room. Grinning, he set down the bucket, pulled back the covers on John's cot, and switched on his flash.

All he could do was gulp.

The black snake was as thick around as his flashlight and easily five feet long—counting coils. In the wavering light it raised its narrow head and flicked its tongue at him warningly.

Charlie's mouth opened in a soundless scream as the overhead light went on.

"Hel-lo-oo, Charlie!" said John. "Say hello to my friend, Ernie!" He came into the room, grinning, and peered into the bucket at the writhing crab. "Nice specimen, but not in the same class, do you think?" He sat down on the side of his bed and picked up the black snake.

"Mom makes me keep him under the house because he's gotten so big, but he wouldn't hurt a kitten. He didn't scare you, did he?"

Charlie shook his head. "No problem," he said, breathing hard.

"That's good." John wound the snake around his waist. "Maybe I'll just smuggle him out the back door before Mom sees him and gets upset." He turned back when he reached the door curtain. "And Charlie?"

"What?"

"I know you can be a little more—more creative, if you put your mind to it. All right?"

"Right," said Charlie. As soon as he heard the back door slam, he grabbed the bucket and ran downstairs to dump the big blue crab into the bay. When he came back into the cottage, Rosie gave him a close look.

"What are you up to, Charlie?"

"Nothing," he said unhappily. That was the trouble. John had him on the edge of a cliff—at the top of a waterfall—standing by the open door of an airplane at thirty thousand feet without a parachute—and he wasn't doing one single solitary thing to keep himself from being pushed over. "Absolutely nothing!"

But that had to change.

Chapter Seven

The next morning he woke up abruptly when something wet and slippery was shoved down the collar of his pajamas. "No!" he screamed in protest. Grabbing the thing by the tail, he bashed it against the side of the bed and threw it across the room.

"Whoa!" John cried. "Don't kill it or its mate will pine away and die." Then he burst out laughing. "Relax, Charlie. It's one of my swim flippers."

Charlie leaned over the side of the bed and stared at the green scuba flipper on the rug. "It was all wet!"

"I know. I ran it under the faucet first."

"Thanks a lot! I thought it was Ernie."

"Snakes don't feel wet. Anyway, Ernie's lots bigger than that. But I wish you could have seen the look on your face, Charlie!"

"John?" Rosie called from the next room. "John? Will you go ask Mom something for me? Or are you still in bed?"

John flung himself back onto the cot, stifling his laughter. "Sorry! I'm still in bed," he said virtuously to the ceiling.

What happened next happened too fast to see. One moment John was lying there grinning. Ten seconds later a long stream of water poured straight down on his face.

"R-R-RO-seee!" he bellowed—and leapt up, coughing and laughing at the same time. "Rosie, you little devil! How did you get up that high?"

"I stood on the dresser. And if you tell Mom what I did, I'll tell her you're still throwing dirty laundry over the wall into my bed. I'll tell her I was just giving you a pitcher of wash water."

"JOH-UNNN!" his mother shouted up the stairs.

"I didn't do anything," John called back. "It was Rosie this time. Honest!"

"Rosie put salt in the sugar bowl?"

John slapped his forehead, stricken. "Oh, no! I did that for Charlie's cereal." He stuck his head out the bedroom door. "Sorry, Mom. I thought you were on a diet again."

"Not during vacation!" Aunt Edie wailed. "For a treat I brewed myself one perfect cup of coffee before I sat down to work—and you made me ruin it."

"Don't grind your teeth, Mom!" Rosie called cheerfully.

"Shut up, and come to breakfast—all of you! Are you still alive, Charlie?"

"Yes." He swung his legs over the side of the bed and went over to the window. The tide was high enough to swim this morning, so at least he didn't have to get dressed. Hurriedly he pulled on his trunks and reached for his tennis shoes. For once, instead of jamming his feet in blindly, he had the wit to shake the shoes first. When he did, a slippery orange blob fell out on the fiber carpet.

"Yu-uck!" went Charlie.

"What's the matter?" Rosie called over the wall.

"John put a mussel in my shoe—a *shelled* mussel," he said in disgust.

"Pop it under his pillow!"

"Don't!" John said from the doorway, his eyes gleaming. "Guess what I saw out the bathroom window? A helicopter just landed up at the point—and a couple of men got out and headed for that white yacht. Come on! Let's go see what's happening."

Charlie just stood there.

"Come on!" John said. "For all we know, this guy is getting all his money from the Mafia. Trust me, Charlie! No garbage. If we go down the road and come up on them from the other side—underneath the pier—they won't even know we're there. All I want to do is get a look at the helicopter, maybe hear what they're saying."

"If he sees you, he'll yell at you!" Rosie warned.

"Let him yell. What about it, Charlie?"

Charlie was only worried about one thing. "What about breakfast?"

"We'll eat on the run."

Ten minutes later, Charlie was jogging along the highway, chomping on doughnuts. It was a bumpy business and he was glad when John finally swerved off the road onto a narrow, overgrown path. "Is this the lane to the pier?" he gasped.

John stopped. "This is the old path. Gangi had a paved road put in when the house was finished, but they'd see us if we went that way."

"Gangi?" Charlie shoved the last doughnut in his mouth and swallowed.

"That's his name. Before he retired he owned a bunch of grocery stores." John stepped out of the underbrush and looked around, then he motioned for Charlie to follow.

"I thought you didn't know anything about him," Charlie whispered. Out in the open he felt as if people were staring at him, but all he could see was empty beach and the sturdy understructure of the pier—each piling banked by a mound of huge rocks.

"I don't. Wait until you see the house, then tell me how many grocery stores it would take to pay for one that big." John gave Charlie a shove. "Go on! Crawl up the embankment and take a look, but don't let them see you."

Charlie stepped on the first rock, then a second. That one tilted, and scattered a spray of small stones downward. He held his breath.

"What are you stalling for?" John hissed.

Licking doughnut sugar off his lips, Charlie moved up three more rocks and stopped. Last year the whole point had been sand and scrub brush—with one big, glorious tide pool in the middle. Now, stretched out before him, was a paved area the size of a downtown parking lot—and, on the far side of it, a big blocky building.

The size was stupefying. There were plenty of windows, but still the place looked more like an overgrown barn than someone's home. The cement parking lot was big enough for a dozen people flying kites, but now it was empty except for the little red helicopter.

"What do you think?" asked John in a low voice, clambering up behind him. "Big enough for you?"

Charlie nodded.

"What are they doing?"

Cautiously, Charlie moved up one more rock. The dory was tied up at the end of the long pier and there were three men standing near it. Maybe they were about to row out to the yacht, maybe not.

"They're on the dock, talking."

"Perfect!" said John. He scrambled down the bank and led the way along the dark alley of shade beneath the pier, walking between the pilings out to the edge of the water and into it.

Charlie waded in after him, trying not to splash—conscious of the voices overhead before he was able to sort out the words. When he made sense of them, it was the man from the train—Mr. Gangi—who seemed to be doing the talking, telling some kind of drawn-out story in his gravelly voice.

"So the second guy took this big plaster elephant foot and made fake tracks in the snow that led right up to the sleeping tent. Then, in the morning, when they all woke up—"

Charlie sneezed. He hadn't felt it coming, but all of a sudden he sneezed. Loud.

After that everything happened at once. John ran, waving for Charlie to follow him, and the three men on the pier began to shout—with Mr. Gangi shouting the loudest of all.

"You kids have had your last warning. Now I'm gonna shoot!"

Up to that point Charlie had been just running. Now he bent low and took off like a Ferrari, racing across the open beach after John.

"Stop!" Mr. Gangi shouted.

The shot made a loud cracking sound.

"Duck!" John cried. Pale under his tan, he pulled

Charlie into the underbrush, then back toward the highway, crashing through the bushes. Behind them, the old man laughed like a hyena and fired again—one, two, three, four more times—making it sound almost merry.

"Oh, no!" John yelled, straightening up in sudden fury. "That's a starting gun, Charlie. For sailboat races! He's firing blanks at us—and laughing his head off!"

Chapter Eight

"Did he yell at you?" Rosie asked when they got back to the cottage.

"He shot at us," John said angrily, keeping his voice low so their mother wouldn't hear.

"Shot at you?"

"It was a starter's gun," Charlie explained. "The kind they use at swim meets. It uses blanks, not real bullets."

"But he laughed at us. They all laughed their heads off and it wasn't the least bit funny, was it, Charlie?"

To his surprise, Charlie found he wasn't sure. Actually, after he knew Gangi wasn't shooting real bullets, it had been sort of nice to see John on the other side of a joke. "Oh, I don't know," he said. "It was just as funny as when I turned back your covers and saw Ernie."

"That's not the same thing. Gangi is a stranger. We figured he was shooting real bullets. But you know me! You know I wouldn't do anything to hurt you."

"Yeah, but I didn't know Ernie," said Charlie. Then he grinned because he'd gotten off a good one. He was sure it was a good one, but John wasn't smiling.

"I don't like being shot at," Charlie tried to explain. "Not even with blanks. But I don't like big snakes either—or rotten tomatoes flying out of drawers—or plastic ice cubes with bugs in them."

John stared at him as if he couldn't believe what he was hearing. "You don't mean you're quitting? Hey, you haven't even started yet."

"Maybe I won't start," Charlie said, relieved.

"You've got to. I've already played ten or fifteen jokes on you."

"But I didn't want you to."

"Well, I *did* want *you* to! We've got a contest going on. Remember? You can't quit, Charlie! You owe me!"

"I can't think of anything to do!" Charlie shouted. "I don't have any ideas, don't you understand?"

"I'll give you some ideas." John grinned, then ran up on the porch and into the cottage, letting the screen door slam behind him.

"What will he do?" Charlie asked with a sigh.

Rosie shook her head. "Like Mom says, 'I shudder to think.' " Then she brightened. "Want to go catch hermit crabs?"

Charlie shook his head. That was too easy. Bash open a mussel and put it in a shallow pool—and in less than a minute five or six hermits would be fighting over the bright orange flesh. "What about the sea anemones?"

"We can't go there! He just shot at you, didn't he?"

"It was a starting gun, I told you. He was trying to be funny," said Charlie. Maybe the old man would be mad. But it wasn't fair that they couldn't go to the point anymore. Bad enough that Gangi had bulldozed the tide pool. There'd been little silver fish in that pool. "On the train he didn't seem all that mean."

"Probably they don't let people yell on trains."

Charlie grinned. "Tell you what! We'll walk right up to the house and tell him we're going to go look at the sea anemones. That way he won't have any reason to yell at us. Come on!"

They ran all the way to the point. If they were going to talk to Gangi, Charlie knew they had to do it fast— before he lost his nerve. Even as they crossed the long green lawn, his steps slowed to a walk.

Rosie looked at him sidewise. "The helicopter's gone. Maybe he went away in it?"

Charlie swung around. The big cement parking lot

was empty, the pier deserted. How come he hadn't noticed? He must be really nervous. Quickly he looked back at the house. No sign of life. Put bars on the windows and the big ugly place could be a prison. But there were no bars—only curtains—and one of them moved as he stared at it.

He stopped dead. Why was he visiting a man who had thrown garbage on him and pretended to shoot him? How was he going to explain about the sea anemones when he didn't even know what they were? What was Rosie going to think when he told her that he'd changed his mind and didn't want to do this?

"This is a dumb idea," she said suddenly, pulling him back. "Let's forget it."

It was what he wanted to do, but it wouldn't solve anything. "No! We'll talk to him," he said firmly, and took the lead again.

The tall front door, carved with scrolls and curlicues, looked as if it had been knocked off an old castle and nailed on the barnlike house. It didn't fit. Rosie and he didn't fit here either. He had to make himself lift the heavy brass knocker.

"FOR HE'S A JOLLY GOOD *FELL*-LOW—"

Charlie flinched. The tune was so insistent he seemed to hear the words as well as the music. "HE'S A JOLLY GOOD *FELLOW*—WHICH NOBODY CAN DEE-NY!"

With hardly a pause, the chimes began to bang out "How Dry I Am"—and then, right in Charlie's face, a

47

six-inch-square section of the oak door opened out and downward on two long chains, like a miniature drawbridge.

"What do you want?" demanded a hoarse voice.

Charlie swallowed. The eyes were all he could see— pale eyes under caterpillar brows—then, abruptly, the chimes stopped and the eyes disappeared. Hardly breathing, he waited for the doorknob to turn.

"READY!" called the familiar hoarse voice—and a small toy cannon rolled out to the edge of the draw- bridge. "AIM! FIRE!"

The last two words came in rapid succession. A thin stream of water arced from the cannon and hit Charlie full in the face. Hard. He spit—and the tall door opened.

"Don't just stand there dripping," said Mr. Gangi with a sly grin. "Come in!"

No way! Charlie decided, and backed up in silent fury. Backed right into Rosie and remembered why he had come. Gritting his teeth, he stepped inside and she followed.

"Care for an umbrella? You know what they say! Better late than never." Mr. Gangi barely touched the elephant-foot umbrella stand just inside the door, and a plastic cobra shot up.

Charlie and Rosie exchanged a pitying glance and walked into the bright living room. Three large win- dows made up most of the east wall. They were like three pictures of the bay—with the moored white yacht centered in the middle frame.

"Have a seat!" With his unlit cigar the old man waved Rosie toward the smaller of the two easy chairs by the fireplace and motioned for Charlie to take the other. They sat down stiffly, not meeting one another's eyes.

"Let's see now," said Mr. Gangi, settling himself on the loveseat across from them. He looked closely at Rosie. "You're the girl who collects fish in jars, and you," he said, and pointed his cigar at Charlie, "you're the one with the rubber glove full of grape juice."

"Grape Kool-Aid," said Charlie.

"How did that trick go?" Mr. Gangi asked, grasping the arm of the loveseat as he leaned forward, alert.

"I blew it." Charlie was trying to decide how much to tell the man when all of a sudden the chair seat rose beneath him and the chair back smacked him from behind. He catapulted through the air and landed on all fours by the hearth.

"Charlie!" Rosie yelled, and leapt out of her own chair.

"I'm fine!" Charlie said quickly. He got up and dusted off his knees, studying the old man's face.

Gangi's pale eyes shone with glee. "That's a little toy I brought home from my novelties factory. An adaptation of the airplane ejection seat for parlor use."

"Not *my* parlor," said Rosie, wrinkling her snub nose.

"I thought you were a grocer?" said Charlie, who had decided not to sit down again.

"That, too." The old man shrugged his big shoulders. "I'm retired from both jobs, but I go in to the factory every few weeks to see what they're doing." He frowned. "Why didn't you like my cobra?"

Rosie snorted. "My brother has a live five-foot black snake."

"Which I ran into in a dark bedroom yesterday," Charlie added.

Mr. Gangi thought about that for a while and decided to pass. "What did you think of my cannon?" he asked next.

"The cannon was all right," Charlie said without enthusiasm—and was surprised at how disappointed the old man was. "It was the starting pistol that really fooled us," he added quickly. "That was good."

Mr. Gangi brightened.

"I liked the drawbridge," Rosie offered.

"Do you want to see the stuff I've got upstairs?" Mr. Gangi stood up, and waved them toward the door with his cigar. "I've got a fishbowl of squirting fish and a baseball that expands—"

"Do you want to see some sea anemones?" Rosie countered.

"What do they do?"

"Eat what they want—dead or alive, glide around

without any fins or feet, get bigger when they need to, and shrink down to a blob when you touch them." She stopped for breath. "And there're some offshore under your pier."

"So that's why you came." The old man looked disappointed again. "No, thanks."

"Is it all right if we go look at them?" Charlie asked quickly.

"Be my guests." With a smile, Gangi followed them to the door and saw them out. As they crossed the long green lawn, he shouted, "Enjoy yourselves!" Then he turned on the underground sprinkling system full force.

The rest of the day was downhill.

The sea anemones wouldn't open up so that Charlie could see what they were like, Aunt Edie was cross because she'd been worried about the two of them—and John had kept his promise. He'd left to do the lobster pots by the time Charlie and Rosie came in from swimming, but he'd been busy while they were in the water. Charlie's beach towel was drenched with vinegar, his comb was gummy with Vaseline, and all his shoelaces were tied together.

When he opened his dresser drawer, his clothes fell out on the floor. Everything he owned fell out, even the white plastic bag that held his kite stuff, and all the rocks he'd picked up on the beach.

"You all right?" Rosie called over the wall when his rock collection hit the floor.

"Couldn't be better," said Charlie through his teeth. He jammed the drawer back into the dresser right side up, and dumped the stuff in by the armload. What he had to remember now was to stay very calm—not let John see that he was getting to him.

John came home in time to set the table for supper and serve the lemonade. Rosie cut the pizza into gooey triangles. Charlie was ready for trouble so he ignored what he thought was a fake plastic ice cube in his glass until the ice actually melted—and he almost swallowed the dead grasshopper floating belly-up in his lemonade.

John smiled.

Charlie made a point of getting to their bedroom early that night, but John had been there before him. Charlie's other sneakers were nailed to the floor, his pajama legs tied in knots, and his dresser drawers upended. With a groan of despair, he threw everything back into the righted drawers and buried his head under the pillow—in a glob of shaving cream.

Chapter Nine

Charlie woke up wishing he'd asked Gangi about flying kites in the big cement parking lot. But he hadn't. Then he realized that there was something resting lightly on his chest. Something weird and slightly smelly. As soon as John stopped whistling around the room and thumped down the stairs, Charlie opened his eyes to see what it was.

An eighteen-inch horseshoe crab shell.

Charlie sighed, and set it on the floor. Very carefully he made a tour of the bedroom. He found raw egg yolk in his left shoe, horseradish on his toothbrush, and all of his socks smelled of perfume. By suppertime he had also discovered that the last four pages of the mystery he was reading had been glued to one another, the sleeves of his favorite shirt sewn together, and the shampoo bottle filled with molasses.

But when he met Aunt Edie in the kitchen at five o'clock, he still hadn't thought of a trick to play on John.

"Since it's your first supper, I thought I ought to show you around," said Aunt Edie. She pushed her glasses up on her forehead. "This, of course, is your basic hamburger meat—untouched by human hands, or by John's—which is more to the point. And in the other corner, ingredients for a tossed salad—lettuce, peppers, tomatoes, cucumbers, and celery. Make of it what you will." She started to leave, then stopped in the doorway. "Poor Charlie, gentle Charlie. Are you sure you want to spend the summer being duped?"

He shrugged. John was right. It wasn't fair to quit when he was losing. But her "untouched by human hands" had given him an idea. As soon as she left, he tore the plastic wrap off the mound of ground beef, whacked it into four portions, and shaped the portions into patties.

Now, what could he put into John's? A marble from the Chinese checkers? No. It wasn't repulsive enough, and anyway John might swallow it. If it weren't for Aunt Edie's rule about not ruining food, he could use hot pepper or soap. As it was, he had to find something that wouldn't fall apart when it was cooked, didn't have any taste, and looked gruesome. Without much hope

54

he wandered around the kitchen, opening drawers filled with linens and cupboards stacked with dishes and closing them again.

The pantry was no better. Nothing but canned goods and Uncle Paul's fishing stuff. He started to close the door again, then stopped. Beyond the row of fishing rods on the far wall was a pegboard—and hanging from the pegboard were his uncle's lures and flies. Bright-colored, grotesque, hairy, furry flies. Charlie grinned and chose one.

Back at the kitchen counter, he worried the fly free of its hook and worked it into the mound of ground meat. By the time the others came in, he had the table set, the salad put together, and all four hamburgers sizzling in the skillet.

"Why didn't you cook them out on the grill?" asked Rosie.

"I never gave it a thought," Charlie answered—which was the truth. All he could think about was how to get the fishing fly hamburger to John without giving himself away.

"I like mine pretty rare," warned Aunt Edie, plate in hand.

"No problem," Charlie said quickly. He slid the pancake turner under one of the browned patties and plopped it on her hamburger bun. One down, three to go.

"Me, too!" said Rosie, at his elbow.

Two and two. Charlie flipped the remaining burgers with care. Now he was up against the wire. Showdown at the old corral—and John was better at bluffing than he was. But John was pretty cocky, too.

"I'm starving," he said, looking over Charlie's shoulder. "That one's done enough for me." He pointed at the hamburger that was pure meat.

"They're both done now," said Charlie, his voice noncommittal, his eyes on the skillet.

"You mean, I can have either one?"

"Sure!" Charlie swallowed. "Whichever one you want."

"How about that?" John's eyes shone. "Decisions, decisions. But I guess I'll still have that one."

Without a word, Charlie slid the pancake turner underneath the pure hamburger and lifted it in the air.

"Wait! The other one's bigger. Why should you get the big one?"

"Because I'm the cook, that's why!"

Smiling triumphantly, John moved his plate away. "Too bad, Charlie. You blew it. I'll take the other one." He watched while the exchange was made, then he sat down at the table. "Hey? Get the ketchup while you're up, Cook!"

No way could he trust John! Charlie took his plate with him to the refrigerator—to be safe—and got out the ketchup.

"And the pickles, too!"

"I don't see any pickles," Charlie objected, his plate in one hand and the ketchup bottle in the other.

"Move!" Rosie pushed him aside and found the pickles behind the orange juice jug.

"Thanks!" said Charlie, uneasy about having both of them away from the table. He knew Rosie didn't think he could trick John, but this time he was going to surprise her.

"Good hamburger!" John said, licking ketchup off his chin. "Don't you think so, Mom?"

Startled, Aunt Edie looked up from her book and bit into her hamburger. "Very good! Not as rare as I ordered, but still juicy." She took another bite—and spit it out in indignation.

"Charlie! How *could* you?"

Charlie and Rosie stared, horror-stricken, at the hairy, blue fly quivering on Aunt Edie's plate—but John burst out laughing. "Charlie! Charlie! Charlie!" he screamed, wiping the tears from his eyes. "You really aren't very good at this sort of thing, are you?"

Chapter Ten

By nine the next morning, all the bounce had gone out of Charlie. He came down the stairs one at a time, stopping at the window on the landing to stare at a rabbit. It was an old rabbit—long in the muzzle and sharp-spined. A bony old rabbit and smart. When he took the next step, it would run.

"Charlie? What was that crash upstairs?"

He moved down one more step. When the rabbit disappeared into the underbrush, he turned to his aunt. She was still dripping after her swim, and her eyes, beneath wet dark lashes, were like Rosie's. "I tripped and fell on my face," he explained.

"Because John tied a string across the door, I suppose." She saw his surprise and sighed. "We've all had a taste of being victim. You, however, hold the record for having the most and meanest tricks played on you in the shortest period of time. Congratulations!"

"Thanks."

"I told John he couldn't play jokes on you when you got here—because he'd gone to such extremes with the rest of us—and then you came along with that stupid rubber glove business."

"Sorry." Charlie didn't want her to see how sorry he really was so he wandered out on the porch.

Aunt Edie followed him, drying her hair on a big striped towel. "I know John's been at loose ends, having Pete gone all summer, but there's no reason to torture the rest of us."

"What's that?" asked Charlie, pointing at what looked like an uninflated air mattress spread out on the grass. A raft maybe? His spirits rose. In his kite book there was a whole chapter on towing rafts with kites—even when there wasn't much wind. "Is that something we can take in the water?"

"Just the opposite!"

"What do you mean?"

"Exactly what I said!" Aunt Edie shook her head vehemently, spraying water on him. "It's a stupid inflatable boat that John bought from Pete's brother. And, since I don't have time to take on a boat in addition to—and anywhere in the vicinity of—three tin-eared children, you may *not* take it in the water— not you, not Rosie, not John. Is that clear?"

"What are you talking about?" asked Rosie, elbowing her way out the screen door with a bowl of cereal in one hand and a glass of juice in the other. "John's boat?"

"Yes, but it isn't John's boat unless your father wants to be responsible for it. If he says it can be kept to use weekends while he's here to watchdog you three, fine! *I* say no one touches it! Not while I'm on guard duty. And that's a hard and fast rule!"

"Rules, schmools," said John, coming out on the porch as his mother went in.

"I mean it!" she called through the screen door. "Foul me up on this one, and you'll fry."

John smiled at the other two. "Is it worth frying for? What are we talking about?"

"Your boat," said Charlie, staring at his cousin. John seemed even more pleased with himself than usual, which meant that something unpleasant was about to happen—happen to Charlie, of course.

He went inside to get breakfast but nothing seemed safe. John was pretty relaxed about his mother's don't-spoil-the-food rule, so he couldn't trust the orange juice or the milk. True, Rosie had used them, but John had come along after that. Charlie reached for a sealed box of Rice Krispies—then he balked. He was thirsty enough to drink an ocean. Good grief! John was making him crazy—changing him into some kind of a freak who was afraid to eat breakfast. Angrily, he went back to the refrigerator—just as the telephone rang.

"It's for you, Charlie!" Rosie called.

Probably it was his mother. He wasn't exactly homesick, but it would be good to talk to her. Not to tell her what was going on. Just to find out how Homer was doing.

"Hello?" he said eagerly.

"This is operator 32," said a nasal male voice. "I am sorry, but we seem to have lost your call. Will you hang up please? We will dial you again as soon as we make the connection."

"All right," said Charlie, puzzled and disappointed at the same time. He hung up the phone.

"Was that your folks?" Rosie asked.

"I don't know. The operator said something about losing the connection. They're going to call back."

"Sounds fishy to me," John said. "How can an operator lose the connection?"

Charlie shook his head, feeling let down. That had to have been his folks trying to reach him.

"Well, you answer if it rings again."

"All right," said Charlie. He went back to the kitchen where Rosie was pouring herself a glass of milk. He waited until she'd drunk some, then he helped himself.

"Want me to taste-test a banana for you, or will you trust the wrapper?" She shook her head at him in despair, then the telephone rang again.

"Phone's ringing!" John shouted from the porch.

Charlie ran to the dining room. "Hello?" he said quickly.

"This is operator 32," said the same voice, sounding even more sing-song and nasal than before. "Is this Charles Michael Martin?"

"Yes," said Charlie eagerly. "Speaking."

"I have a message for you. Do you have a pencil?"

"Yes," said Charlie, breathing faster. He picked up the pen and pulled the pad of paper closer.

"Are you ready, sir?"

"Yes! Go ahead!" Charlie pressed down the pen to make sure it worked and the stupid thing buckled as if it were made of licorice. Drat John! Dad might want him to phone at the office and he didn't have that number. "Hold on!" he said. "Wait'll I get a pen that writes."

"Sorry, sir. Your time is up," said the sing-song voice. "To remove the telephone receiver from your ear, pull gently but firmly to separate it from the instant glue, then go soak your head in soapy water."

Pete's brother. Only John could have set him up this way—so the voice on the phone had to be Pete's brother. That idiot John! What next? Was there nothing he wouldn't try to get Charlie to pull a joke on him? That stupid pen! That whiny operator! How did he get people to do things like that?

"Charlie?" said Rosie. "Are you giggling?"

"I can't—I can't help it!" gasped Charlie, bent over with laughter. "Go soak your head, he said! How does he come up with dumb things like this over and over again? How can he keep it up?" Without thinking, he pulled the receiver away from his ear and then caught his breath.

"Yu-uck!" Rosie cried out. "Your ear is bleeding!"

"I know," Charlie said softly. "But I'm going to take care of it. Trust me, Rosie! Now I'm really going to take care of it."

Chapter Eleven

It was hard to figure. This business with the telephone was the one joke that had struck him funny, but it was the last straw. He'd had enough. What could he do that would make all of John's tricks look like kindergarten pranks—like third-rate, gimcrack prizes from Cracker Jack boxes? He had to play the worst practical joke in the world on John—and do it before dark today.

"Here!" said Rosie, and handed him a paper towel. She watched him staunch the blood without saying anything, then she grinned. "Want to make some kites and go fly them out at Beavertail? The wind'll be wild, but the park ranger can help us if we get them caught on the lighthouse."

Charlie looked at her in despair. Of course, he wanted to go to Beavertail. He wanted to fly kites, and look for egrets in the marsh, and climb the high rocks across from Gould Island, and reread *Watership Down*. He wanted to do all the things that he and Rosie did together every summer—but first he had to take care of John.

"I can't," he said.

"You never can! You don't do anything that's fun anymore. You might as well not even be here this summer." She studied him in exasperation. "I told you—the only thing to do about John is ignore him. *Why* can't you go to Beavertail?"

"I'm going to be busy," he said grimly.

"Me, too," said John through the screen door. "I'm off to help Ed paint buoys. See you guys at supper."

Rosie groaned. "I forgot! He cooks tonight. What poisonous thing can you do with chicken wings?"

Charlie shrugged.

"Well, I offered to fly kites. Remember that!" said Rosie, and banged out the door.

She was mad now, but it wouldn't last. Rosie didn't hold grudges. Anyway, he needed to be alone to concentrate. The furry fishing lure had almost worked, but he'd had to search the kitchen inch by inch to come up with the idea. So the best thing to do was go over the rest of the cottage the same way—starting with the dining room.

The bookcase had a double row of books on each shelf, and a stack of place mats on top. The only other furniture—besides the dining room table and chairs—was a built-in sideboard. The top cupboard was full of dishes, and the bottom one turned out to be crammed with dusty old vases. But the drawer between held treasure.

Charlie smiled. In a nest of chewed-up paper, four tiny hairless mice huddled together blindly. His fingers itched to touch them, but he knew better. Uncle Paul always said that mice mothers might not feed their babies again if they smelled people on them. It was Uncle Paul who had started them calling all the mice Belinda. "Whoops!" he'd say. "There's Belinda scooting up the chimney." Or, when he'd gone to the kitchen to help bring in dessert, "Whoops! There goes Belinda behind the hot water heater."

The back door slammed. Charlie closed the drawer carefully and turned around. If it was Rosie, he would show her the mice.

But it was Aunt Edie—her arms full of brown paper bags. "Charlie! I thought everyone was out." Her cheeks were flushed, and she seemed embarrassed. "I was just bringing in a few things from the back of the car."

Surprised, he looked at the open study door. He hadn't heard her leave—hadn't noticed that the typewriter was no longer clattering.

She let her packages slide onto the table, smiling at him. "I guess I can trust you. You know what happens next week, don't you?"

He shook his head, bewildered.

"The Fourth of July, silly! I have to stash these fireworks while John is out of the house—just ladyfingers and sparklers—and a few rockets. Your Uncle Paul will set those off. Lift the lid on the cedar chest for me, will you, Charlie?"

He went into the living room and did as she asked, first moving a pile of raincoats and slickers.

Aunt Edie dropped in the paper bags. Then she closed the lid of the chest and put the coats back on top. "Thanks," she said. "You won't mention the fireworks to the others, will you, Charlie?"

"No," he said, trying hard to stay calm. Or, at least, to look calm. "I promise." He waited for her to close the study door. When the typewriter started up again, he threw the raincoats on the floor, propped the chest open, and started rooting through the brown paper bags.

Kaa-booom! That was what he needed. A big noise without much damage. So what should he choose? With rockets, he couldn't be sure how much powder he was getting, but ladyfingers were only pop-pop-pop-pop. They didn't amount to much, but if he put a batch together he could make an impression on John without hurting him. Very carefully he snapped off one series of ladyfingers, then a couple more—and stuffed them in his pockets. After he'd jammed the rest back and closed the chest, he went out on the porch, gulping for breath.

All right. He'd gotten away with stealing the stuff. Now what should he do with it? Even if he figured out how to make a bomb, where could he put it? John wouldn't be home until four-thirty or five. Just in time to fix supper. The sooner after that that it happened—and the farther away from Aunt Edie that it happened—the better. Since she usually came into the kitchen about five to lay out the food for that night's cook, the best bet would seem to be either the spare bedroom upstairs, or the upstairs bathroom.

Charlie sat down on the porch steps and stared at the beach. He had to think. No one used the spare bedroom until his folks got here in August. But the bathroom? That might work because John always ran upstairs to wash after he came in from lobstering. But what kind of a booby trap could he set up there that Rosie wouldn't trigger before her brother got home?

Then the idea came to him. It was so obvious, so simple. Charlie smiled—and went back inside to get to work.

Chapter Twelve

At five minutes to five, Aunt Edie was still in her study and John hadn't come home yet. From the lounger on the porch, Charlie searched the horizon for Pete's brother's green trawler.

"He'd better get back in time to fix supper," Rosie said. "That's one thing Mom is strict about." She gave Charlie a close look. "You're not planning anything that will keep us from eating on time, are you? I'm hungry."

Charlie grinned. She didn't have any faith in him, didn't think he could play a trick that worked—one that wouldn't backfire—but this time he had a winner. Finally he had dreamed up a practical joke that would make believers out of all of them.

The back door slammed. Of course. They'd docked at Pete's place and John must have come home by way of the road. But he was running late. Suppose he decided to wash up in the kitchen?

For the next forty seconds Charlie leaned back in the lounger and tried to make his muscles relax. John had to go upstairs. He *had* to use the upstairs bathroom.

"Hello!" John called, waving through the big screen doors. "Running a little late but I'll be right back down," he said to his mother as she came out of her study.

It was going to work. He never should have doubted it. This very minute Aunt Edie was on her way to the kitchen and John was tearing up the steps. The times were going to mesh. But what if the noise was still too loud?

Charlie sat forward and began to fiddle with the little portable radio on the table beside him. John's radio. Music, loud music—that was what he needed. He found a rock station and turned up the sound. He could sense Rosie watching him—wondering if he'd lost his mind—but he didn't dare look at her. If it was going to happen, it had to happen soon.

It did.

The explosion was spectacular. For at least ten seconds the sounds from the loud rock station were obliterated. Rosie flew out of her deck chair and Aunt Edie ran out on the porch with the binoculars.

"What happened? Who's shooting?" she demanded, raising the glasses. "Is it another one of those tests?" She combed the bay with her binoculars.

Charlie shaded his eyes and pretended to stare out at the water, but Rosie, open-mouthed, looked only at Charlie. Then, overhead, John slammed down the toilet seat—and Aunt Edie caught on.

She lowered the glasses and looked hard at the porch ceiling as if she expected to see through it to whatever had happened in the second-floor bathroom. Then she turned to Charlie. "Was the noise I just heard made by what I think it was made by?"

Charlie nodded guiltily, not meeting her eyes.

"What exactly did you do?"

He swallowed. "I booby-trapped the toilet seat."

Chapter Thirteen

John was white around the mouth when he came downstairs—and Aunt Edie was just getting warmed up.

"I consider this a breach of trust, Charlie. You *promised* me."

"I promised not to tell anyone."

"Don't quibble!" she shouted.

"Why the devil did you put a bomb under the toilet seat—of all places?" demanded John.

"Because I didn't want Rosie or your mother to—"

"Don't any of you expect fireworks this year because I'm going to soak whatever's left in the bathtub and throw it in the garbage. You can just forget about the Fourth of July!"

"Hey? That's not fair!" said John. "I didn't even

know you had fireworks. It was Charlie who made the bomb."

"You drove him to it," said his mother, shaking the binoculars at him. "Which reminds me of the other thing I wanted to say. From this moment on, no one— I repeat—absolutely no one will play any kind of practical joke, or trick, or anything remotely similar to one, on these premises. Is that understood?"

All three of them nodded.

"Good! Because I have not done a decent day's work since we picked up Charlie at the train station. Mind you, I am not saying that this is all Charlie's fault," she added, as John opened his mouth. "The point is, I have a deadline and I intend to meet it. I want to earn my degree and go back to the real world of teaching other people's children how to read. Is that clear?"

Again they nodded.

"All right. Go fix supper. No more taking turns. All three of you are responsible for all of the meals. All of the time. Work it out and work together. And call me when it's ready."

She went inside. A moment later the study door slammed.

Rosie looked at both boys, obviously uneasy. "I'll set the table," she offered.

"All right," said John. "How did you make that bomb?" he asked Charlie as the two of them followed Rosie into the kitchen.

"Ladyfingers."

"Ladyfingers? How many?"

"I'm not sure." Charlie reddened. "I took the powder out of a couple of batches, but I didn't use it all. I sort of—guessed."

"*Guessed?* Crimeny, Charlie! I could sue! You don't know the first thing about explosives, do you? Do you realize what you could have done to me?"

The study door opened. "And don't bicker," said Aunt Edie. "Get into that kitchen. NOW!"

Supper was very quiet. Even cleaning up after supper was quiet. John put the leftover food away, Charlie carried the dirty dishes to the kitchen, and Rosie wiped off the table and put away the place mats. Then John washed and the other two dried.

After that they played Monopoly, the way they had when they were younger. But this time Rosie didn't scream when she landed on Park Place, and John didn't try to keep the game going by forcing loans on them when Charlie and Rosie were mortgaged to the hilt.

Going to bed was the strangest of all. It wasn't just that John didn't throw his dirty socks over the wall into Rosie's room—or that Charlie wasn't worried about finding an eel under his pillow. It was the silence.

The only sound in the whole cottage was Aunt Edie's typewriter.

Chapter Fourteen

Charlie knew it was morning before he opened his eyes because he could hear the gulls screaming. Then the telephone rang, and there were hurried footsteps on the stairs. Aunt Edie's footsteps.

"John?" she said from their doorway. "Charlie? Wake up! Wake up, Rosie! That was your Aunt Emily on the phone."

John groaned and sat up. "Don't tell me, let me guess. She's dropping off the twins for you to babysit, and *we* have to do it so you can work on your paper."

"Worse! Your grandmother just broke her wrist and Emily is driving her to the hospital. Mrs. Walker—Emily's neighbor—is with Jeremy and Joshua now, but I have to get to Providence by eight-thirty to take over."

"Why? I mean, why by eight-thirty?" asked Rosie from the next room.

"Because that's when Mr. Walker has to leave for work. They don't want the twins near their new baby because Jeremy has strep throat."

John lay back and closed his eyes. His mother poked at his cot with her bare foot. "Pay attention, John! I need to talk to you before I go."

"Fat lot of good that will do!" called Rosie.

"How true, how true," John murmured, his eyes still closed.

Maybe it was just as well, Charlie decided, pushing back his blanket. Not Gram breaking her wrist, but Aunt Edie having to drive into Providence today. Maybe all this confusion would make her forget about yesterday.

"All right," said Aunt Edie, raising her voice so that Rosie would be sure to hear in the next room. "I'm only going to say this once. I don't want to leave you three behind—especially after what happened yesterday." She paused, and Charlie kept his eyes on his stomach. "But unlike the twins, you are perfectly capable of taking care of yourselves—which is all I'm asking you to do. Please don't do anything stupid until I get back. Promise me?"

"I promise," said Rosie, sounding resigned.

"So do I," said Charlie, without hope.

"Sure! Why not?" John said cheerfully.

Aunt Edie frowned at him. "Remember, you're the

oldest. *Please* take care of the others. I'll be back as soon as I can—four hours, five at the most." She ran down the stairs and a few minutes later Charlie heard the station wagon start up and pull away.

"Four, maybe five hours. Plenty of time," said John, rolling over and pulling the covers over his face. His voice was muffled, but Charlie could make out what he said. "Plenty of time for a nap before I decide how to revenge myself on the mad bomber."

Oh, great! thought Charlie. More to come. Lamebrain that he was, he'd figured the jokes were over. Sure, he'd made a mess of his part, but Aunt Edie had finally stopped the stupid contest. Except that she hadn't. John didn't sound slowed down—let alone stopped—promise or no promise. And Aunt Edie had gone off and left them. Now what was he going to do?

Not fall back to sleep. Very carefully he reached for his shorts and began to squirm into them.

Then, from under the covers, John made a soft noise that was half snore and half snort.

Charlie froze. When the breathing in the other cot was even again, he zipped his shorts and reached for his sneakers.

"Pssst!" went Rosie through the knothole. "Are you asleep?"

He leaned close to the wall and barely breathed it. "No."

"Let's get out of here!"

As he finished tying his shoes, she joined him on the porch—carrying a package of cinnamon buns. "Let's go out on the big rock," she said, looking up at the ceiling warily. "For some reason I don't trust John."

"Did you hear what he said? About revenge?"

She nodded. "It figures. You really shook him up."

"Hey, he wanted me to do something. He *asked* for it!"

"I didn't say he didn't. Just don't expect him to stop there."

They circled the barbecue chimney and slid down the huge, sloping rock on the seat of their pants, Rosie cradling the cinnamon buns in her arms. The tide was low enough so that they could work their way down to the bottom ledge, out of sight of the cottage, and sit with their legs dangling over the water.

"He promised to stop there," Charlie said with his mouth full of bun.

Rosie shook her head, and swallowed. "No, he didn't. Mom never remembers that John's mind works like a lawyer's. All she made us promise was not to do anything stupid. Remember? And one person's 'stupid' is another person's 'brilliant.' "

"But yesterday she said that none of us could play any more tricks," he said, reaching for the last bun. "Remember that?"

"I told you. She's not very good at that sort of thing. *Then* she added 'on these premises.' Right?"

"Right," said Charlie, glummer still. Maybe he would have been safer in bed.

"You know what?" Rosie said without moving. "He wasn't really asleep. I'll bet he wanted us to leave so he could lock us out."

She was probably right. She knew how John's mind worked better than anyone, thought Charlie. He and Rosie scrambled up the rock and peered around the barbecue pit. But the dining room door was open as usual. They could see the droopy flowers on the table through the screen.

"I was wrong, I guess," said Rosie, surprised.

"Maybe he hasn't thought of it yet," said Charlie. He was tempted to go back into the cottage, but who wanted to be trapped inside on a day like this? "Maybe I'll just sneak in and get my kite stuff. Do you want anything?"

Rosie considered. "The back door key's hanging on a nail in the kitchen. I'll get it just to be safe. Come on, let's go in that way."

But when they got to the back door, it was closed. Closed and locked tight.

"I knew it!" said Rosie.

They tore around to the front, Charlie in the lead. Aunt Edie locked the dining room door anytime they all left the cottage, but the big screen doors between the front porch and the living room were only hooked together. If they could slip a piece of cardboard between and jiggle the hook—

There was a long, loud, grating sound—and, almost at once, another like it.

Rosie knew what had happened. "Don't do it, John! Don't you dare!" she yelled.

John had pushed back the screen doors and rolled out the massive wooden storm doors in their place. When they ran up on the porch, they heard the rusty bolt slide closed.

"Don't feel lonely, you guys!" John called through the crack. "I'm just 'securing the premises.' I'll be out in a minute to keep you from getting bored."

Chapter Fifteen

"What'd I tell you?" said Rosie. "Off the premises anything goes. He'll probably take after you with the clam rake."

Charlie gave her a startled look.

"Well, it is your own fault. All you've done since you got here is dig yourself in deeper. I told you not to start with him." She sighed. "I don't know. Maybe you ought to run away and hide until Mom comes back?"

Charlie shook his head. That wouldn't be any use. Even if he stayed out of reach until Aunt Edie got home, he'd only be buying time. John would get him eventually—unless he got John first.

That was it, of course. If he wanted to end this

dumb feud, he had to do what Aunt Edie had told him not to do. Play one more trick.

"Where are you going?" Rosie said in alarm.

"Back to the rock," said Charlie, who was already halfway to the sea wall.

"Come with me! Maybe we could walk to Beaver-tail?"

"No, I have to think." Think up something that would put John off practical jokes for the rest of his life.

Down on the bottom ledge again, he stretched flat out on the skinny shelf of rock. About a half mile offshore an old fishing boat moved across the bay slowly in a cloud of gulls. Then along came a second boat—smaller, trimmer. Charlie propped himself up on one elbow and studied it. It was Gangi's white yacht, making a fancy turn as if its owner were showing off—then swinging toward its own sheltered cove at the point.

If only he could get ahold of the mechanism for one of those chairs that shot people across the room. But probably even that wouldn't impress John. If Charlie's bomb hadn't stopped him, what would?

He watched while Gangi anchored the boat and groped his way down the ladder to the dory. Funny old man with his houseful of tricks. He was worse than John.

"Charlie!"

He looked up to see Rosie's face upside down above him.

"What's the matter?" Charlie asked, half blinded by the sun.

"John's going out in the boat."

"The boat?"

"The boat he bought from Pete's brother, stupid! The one that Mom said none of us could touch until Dad came for the weekend. I didn't think he could get it inflated but he did. There's a pump."

"Oh, no!" said Charlie, and scrambled up the rock.

John was dragging the inflated canoe across the lawn on an old blanket. When he saw Charlie coming, he waved. "Want to give me a hand with this?"

"No!"

John smiled, and dragged the boat over to the sea wall. "Get down on the beach and I'll ease it over the edge to you."

"No!" Charlie said again. "Your mom said not to touch it."

"No, she didn't. Not exactly." John ran down the steps himself and pulled the blanket, boat and all, down to the ground. "You've got a good memory, Rosie. What was it Mom said?"

Rosie groaned, suddenly remembering. "She said, not while *she* was on guard duty."

"That's it! That's exactly how she put it. The hard

and fast rule," John said happily, and began to drag the boat toward the water—winding his way around the big rocks.

"But you know what she meant," Rosie called after him. "And you know why she said it. It's not safe, John! That thing's not big enough for the bay—and besides it's dumb to go out alone on a boat."

"Who said I was going alone?" John ran up on the porch and came back with the paddle. "How about it, Charlie? You heard her. We're not even disobeying orders. Want to go for a ride?"

Charlie shook his head. When John saw he wouldn't go, maybe he'd give up the notion.

"Come on, Charlie! Just a nice boat ride. Plenty of time for my vengeance when we get back. I promise not to drown you."

"You'd probably drown both of us!"

"All right! Stay here where it's nice and safe," John said, losing his temper. He waded into the water, pushing the little canoe toward the submerged rock that they sometimes dove from. "I'll drown myself."

At first it looked as if he would—and would do it then and there fifteen yards from shore—but finally John managed to belly-flop himself into the boat and push off.

"Now what?" said Rosie, after he'd paddled away without even looking back. "We could call the coast guard except we can't get into the house."

"He'd kill us! If he didn't drown, he'd kill us for calling the coast guard. What about Pete's brother? Is their house close by?"

"Yes, but they've all gone to Newport for the sailboat races. Ed's uncle is doing the lobster pots—which is why John doesn't have to help."

"Gangi!" said Charlie suddenly. Why hadn't he thought of him right away? He had a boat. He'd even just had it out. "Come on! He can handle John."

Rosie hesitated. "Gangi's pretty strange."

"He's perfect!" said Charlie. He could see she wasn't so sure, but he knew he was right. "Wait here, if you'd rather, and keep an eye on John. I'll go tell Mr. Gangi what's happened."

Chapter Sixteen

He ran as fast as he could. As he got closer he saw that he was in luck. The old man hadn't gone into the house yet—he was just tying up the dory. When Charlie came pounding along the dock, he looked up, interested.

"Hey!" Charlie called, fighting to get his breath. "Your boat— Will—you—take—out—your—boat —again?"

"What for?"

Charlie panted, gasped for air. What if the man wouldn't help him? "My cousin—he took—a—little boat out. An inflatable canoe."

"How old is he?"

"Not quite twelve. And—my aunt's gone away."

"Get in!" said the old man, untying the line again.

Charlie stopped worrying and clambered into the dory. Gangi got in after him and started the outboard motor. "Is this the cousin you tried to play the rubber glove trick on?" he asked over the engine sound.

"Yes."

"The boy who matched you up with a five-foot black snake?"

Charlie nodded. "He likes jokes."

"You go first," Gangi said when they got out to the yacht.

While the old man tied the dory's line to the heavy metal ring on the buoy, Charlie started climbing. Midway up the side of the boat, the rope ladder jerked under him and grew taut. When he tumbled into the cockpit, Gangi was right on his heels.

"Do you like my boat?" he asked, grinning like a little boy.

"Yeah, sure," said Charlie. He stepped to the front of the cockpit. The dory had bounced around on the water like a beach ball but *The Gangi Grocer* was solid. Solid and shiny. All polished brass and gleaming wood. "I don't see him anywhere," he said worriedly, searching the horizon for an orange canoe.

Gangi handed him the binoculars and switched on the ignition. Charlie grabbed the railing as the yacht lurched into motion, steadying the glasses against his eyes. By the time the old man had tuned down the engine noise to a loud buzz, he had found John. "There!" he said excitedly, pulling at Gangi's elbow and pointing.

With a nod, Gangi changed direction slightly and headed toward the little orange speck midway between their shore and Gould Island.

As the yacht got closer, Charlie raised the binoculars again and brought John into focus—waiting for the moment when his cousin recognized him. John was going to be pretty surprised to see him on the white yacht. He didn't even know that Rosie and Charlie had been inside the big house at the point. Didn't know about all of Gangi's tricks and gadgets. Neither he nor Rosie had said anything at home—maybe because of the way they'd ended up under the sprinklers.

John saw them coming all right. At first all he did was paddle faster, but the next time he glanced over his shoulder he seemed to look right at Charlie. He had to recognize him at this range. Charlie lowered the glasses and waved. John turned halfway around and waved back. Jauntily.

"Seems pretty cool so far. Maybe a little green around the gills," Gangi shouted in Charlie's ear. "Want me to turn off the engine and throw him a line?" Suddenly he frowned. "Wait a minute! That dingbat isn't even wearing a life preserver! Doesn't he know that dinky boat could get swept under the bridge and out to sea?"

Charlie shrugged helplessly.

"He needs to be taught a lesson, that's what he needs," the old man said angrily, chewing on his damp cigar. "Maybe we ought to give him a good scare before we pick him up."

"What do you mean?" asked Charlie, wary. He watched the orange speck get smaller as *The Gangi Grocer* made a still wider circle around the little inflatable boat. Right up to the moment when John had waved, Charlie had been afraid for him. But seeing him so—so—cocky had changed that. "What kind of a scare?"

"I'm thinking," Gangi said, grinning. "These jokes he plays? Are you always the chump?"

"Most of the time. But not always," Charlie said, eying the man at the wheel speculatively. It was almost as if Gangi could see into his mind. As if the old man knew that less than an hour ago Charlie had been beating his brains to find the perfect trick to play on John.

"Take the wheel!" Gangi said suddenly.

Charlie shook his head. He didn't want to steer.

"Go on, take it! Just hold her straight for a minute," Gangi said loudly, and moved away.

Charlie let the binoculars hang from his neck, and grabbed for the wheel. At first the throbbing power of the big boat, the wind in his face made him dizzy. They were headed back now and even without the glasses he could see John clearly again. His cousin's body, bent double, was rigid. The paddle was resting on his knees and his eyes were fixed on the yacht barreling toward him.

Why didn't Gangi come back?

"Hold it steady!" the old man shouted from behind him. "Swerve and you'll run him over!"

"We'd better turn!" Charlie yelled. "You take it and turn!" He sucked in his breath. He could see the V-shaped burst of spray from their prow showering over the little orange boat—see the look of fear on John's face as the canoe rose and then dropped, sprang up and fell again like a roller coaster. John gripped the sides of the boat, struggling to ride out the waves. Then, as the yacht swept past, Gangi threw a bucketful of something over the side—and dropped the empty container at Charlie's feet.

He stared down at it aghast. The bucket stank. "You dumped garbage on him!" he said accusingly.

"Fish heads! From the bait cooler," the old man shouted in his ear. "Move over, I'll take it."

Gratefully, Charlie gave up the wheel.

Gangi smiled at him. "Now, what I'm going to do next is run this remote controlled—"

"Go back!" screamed Charlie, who was looking through the glasses again.

"What is it?"

"Gulls! They're going for him the way they do fishing boats. Go back fast!"

The old man swung the yacht around and revved up the engine. Charlie saw the flock of birds circling the canoe in a dark mass, saw their shadows on the water. John was scooping up the bait with his hands, shoveling it over the sides, sloshing water over the little boat to wash it clean, but the gulls were still coming. As *The Gangi Grocer* drew near, one broke away from the rest and swooped down on the bucket at Charlie's feet. It was a big bird—a powerful bird with blank, bright eyes and a cruel beak—and he could feel the force of its wings.

"Get away!" Charlie yelled. "GET AWAY!" he screamed, waving his arms, as the yacht drew near the canoe. The gulls rose in a cloud with a beating of wings, then swooped down again after the white yacht had passed.

But the old man had the starter pistol ready. A shot cracked. The sound of it bounced across the water and this time the flock of gulls flew away. When Charlie looked back, he saw John flat on his face in the bottom of the canoe.

"That'll do it for the birds," said Gangi with a satisfied smile. "Take the wheel again for a minute while I put the shark overboard."

Chapter Seventeen

The old man was crazy. "What do you mean, shark?" Charlie demanded as he took over the steering again.

"The other half of the trick."

"He doesn't need anything more. You've already taught him a lesson."

"He hasn't learned a thing. He's just mad." Gangi grinned around the unlit cigar. "Anyway, the gulls were a mistake. Those fish heads were for shark bait," he said as he left.

Definitely crazy, decided Charlie, taking the white yacht in another wide circle. He'd swum in this water every summer since he'd first learned how to swim. Everyone swam here—on this side and on the Newport side. There just plain weren't any sharks in Narragansett Bay. Gangi had to be putting him on. But, if it weren't true, what was the point of the bait?

"Now we're in business!" said the old man, beside him again, rubbing his hands in anticipation. "This'll shake him up!"

Charlie gave up the wheel. "What will?"

"My shark! I told you. Remote controlled." Gangi proudly held up the tiny radio. "I just put him in the water."

"Not a *toy* shark?" said Charlie, almost relieved. "That'll never fool John."

"Wanna bet?"

"Where is it?"

Gangi turned the boat slightly without increasing its speed. "Right off the prow. See? Headed straight for your cousin. I'm going to make it go around him the way we've been doing—but closer in."

"I don't see anything," said Charlie. Then he did. He saw the black dorsal fin cutting through the water just like in the movie, *Jaws*. His fingers tightened on the railing. "It looks real."

The old man at the wheel chuckled. "I know," he said. "It's a good one. Watch this!"

It took Charlie a few minutes to focus the binoculars on the thin black fin. First it moved north, then in a straight line toward shore, then it made for the bridge—always with the orange canoe at the center of its journeyings. John spotted it in the last quarter of its course, when it was passing between him and the yacht.

Charlie knew when it happened. Knew exactly when tall, handsome, sure-of-himself John first saw the shark. He was just sitting there, scowling at *The Gangi Grocer*, then all of a sudden he stiffened and almost stood up in the boat. He raised the paddle but he couldn't seem to lower it into the water, couldn't take his eyes off the black fin.

Each time the fin went around the little boat it came nearer to it. John was paddling now, pushing himself hard, jerkily switching the paddle from one slippery hand to the other. His face was red, his eyes wild. He kept looking over his shoulder to see where the shark was—how fast it was coming.

Charlie swallowed hard. This was no good. Not what he wanted. Having all those tricks played on him had been bad, but seeing John in a panic—with the whites of his eyes showing and the laughter gone out of him—was worse. He couldn't stomach it. He had to stop it. He wanted John back the way he'd always been. "That's enough!" he yelled to Gangi. "He's scared. He's scared enough!"

"Not yet!" said the old man happily, adjusting the controls on the tiny radio. "Now we'll close in."

The circle narrowed still more. John twisted back and forth in the boat, rocking it, trying to watch the shark. The black fin got closer and closer and John's thrashings grew wilder.

"That's enough!" Charlie shouted again. "He'll capsize it!"

"Want me to pull him in?" asked Gangi.

"YES!"

Then John stood up—and the canoe flipped over.

"HELL-LP!" John bellowed, and went under kicking.

Chapter Eighteen

Gangi laughed so hard he cried. "Hey?" he yelled over the railing. "Hey? We're fishing for sharks. Have you seen any down there?"

John threw him a shocked look and lunged for the bobbing canoe. The boat had righted itself in seconds, but every time he grabbed it, it shot out of his hands. Finally he trapped it against the side of the yacht and hung on.

"Good catch!" cheered the old man, still snorting with laughter. "Watch out below!"

The rope end smacked against the water. Wiping the spray from his eyes, John tied the line to the little boat. Then Gangi dropped the ladder over the side.

"Now grab hold of that shark and get your tail up here!"

John, on the first rung of the rope ladder, bent his head back to look daggers at the old man.

"Go on, do it! He's right behind you!" Gangi urged.

All Charlie could do was cringe when the black dorsal fin nudged the older boy in the small of the back.

"Yee-OWWW!" With a shrill shriek, John flew out of the water.

"Did you see that?" Gangi howled with glee. "Shot from a cannon—then he dropped like a lead sinker! Did you see him?"

John came up sputtering mad. He dove at the fin and swam back to the ladder with it. When he tumbled into the cockpit, he tossed the curved plastic blade at Gangi's feet.

The old man furrowed his black caterpillar brows. "What were you doing in a dinky boat like that without a life jacket?" he thundered.

As far as Charlie could tell, John didn't even hear the man. Once he'd let go of the fin, he stood there dazed, looking blankly at the deck as if he weren't sure what to do next. There was smushed fish head in his hair and blood on his neck where one of the birds had pecked him. Charlie turned away, embarrassed.

Gangi plucked the bit of fish from John's hair, looking a little sheepish. "Sorry about the gulls. Never figured that would happen. I just tossed that bucket of stuff at you to make it look good. Realistic. You know? Bait for the shark?"

John gave him a dark look. Then he gave Charlie a blacker one. "I didn't know you were going to get *him* to help."

"Pete's brother helped you," Charlie said quickly.

"That's not the same thing. Ed's no better at practical jokes than you are. I had to tell him exactly what to say on the phone. But that shark—" He shook his head over and over again. "I *knew* it couldn't be real. It had to be a fake. Nobody ever said anything about sharks around here, and, believe me, I used to ask all the time. I was dead sure it was a joke—until I got thinking. You guys had almost run me down with your big fat yacht and then you threw dead fish at me. For all I knew, someone had brought a live shark here in a barrel." He scowled in Gangi's direction. "I mean, the stupid thing looked so real, I couldn't *not* believe in it."

The old man's face broke into a big smile. "He's a good shark, isn't he? How about my new boat?" he said, gesturing around the cockpit with the cigar. "Do you like my boat?"

"Yeah! Sure!" John's answer was perfunctory, then his eyes brightened as they moved around the white yacht. "It's all right, I guess." He ran his fingers idly over the wood paneling. "I've always wanted to ride on a boat like this. How does she handle?"

"Like a Porsche," Gangi said. "Smooth as silk. Hold on, and I'll show you." He peered over the edge to make sure the canoe was tied fast, then he switched on the ignition and started the engine. This time Charlie knew enough to steady himself as the yacht shot forward.

"You want to take the wheel?" Gangi shouted to John.

"You bet!"

The old man stepped aside, chewing happily on his cigar. He beckoned for Charlie to come closer. "You boys like to go on a boat trip with us Sunday? My wife, Angie, is gonna make a big picnic—sausages, fried chicken, the works. We're taking *The Gangi Grocer* on her first cruise."

"Where to?" asked John, his eyes glowing.

"Well, I'll tell you," said the old man expansively. "I mean to take her under the bridge past Rose Island—" He broke off, staring at the shoreline, then he took the binoculars from Charlie and studied it more closely. "Looks like you've got someone waiting for you at your place."

John snatched the glasses from him and gave a low, unhappy whistle. Even without binoculars, Charlie recognized the tall figure pacing up and down the beach in a seersucker business suit. It was Uncle Paul—and he looked grim.

"Mom must have called him from Providence," John said softly. "Oh, boy! He looks mad enough to spit nails."

Grinning broadly, Gangi cut the motor. "This is as close as I can take you. It's shallow the rest of the way." Neither boy moved, so he thrust his face in John's and spoke distinctly. "Maybe you'd better try steering some other time?"

John was startled but he got ahold of himself and turned to Charlie. "What do you say? Should we go for a little ride first? Give him time to cool down?"

John was out of his mind. His dad was only going to hot up more. The longer they waited, the worse it was going to be. Charlie moved to the railing. "Go on, if you want to. I can paddle back from here. I'd rather get it over with."

John's eyes danced. "He'll boil you in oil."

"Not me, he won't," Charlie said, laughing.

"If you talked to him first, you could sort of explain things?"

"Maybe," answered Charlie, not sure he could. He scrambled down the rope ladder and dropped lightly into the bouncy little canoe.

"Hold on!" Gangi leaned over the railing and tossed him a life jacket. "What about Sunday? Want to come?"

"No, thanks! I'm going to be busy," Charlie said cheerfully, buckling on the life jacket. Then he remembered something important. "Say? Would it be all right if sometimes I flew a kite from that cement lot back of your house?"

"Flew a kite?" The old man shrugged. "Why not? Go ahead." Then he raised the binoculars and studied the shoreline again. "That is not a happy man," he announced loudly.

"Maybe I'll go now after all," John said suddenly. "Wait for me, Charlie!"

"*You* wait!" said Gangi, and handed him a life jacket, too.

John made a face, but he put it on. "I'll bring them back Sunday, if I'm still alive," he said, grinning. "What time?"

"Ten o'clock sharp. My dock," said the old man.

John set the canoe spinning as he landed, but Charlie only laughed. He plunged the paddle into the bright blue water and pulled it toward him—laughing again as the light little boat sprang forward. Right side, left side, right, left, he chanted under his breath, loving the rhythm of it and the liveliness of the little canoe. "Do you know that we could probably pull a boat this size with a kite?" he said to cheer up John.

"This boat won't get wet again this summer," John said gloomily.

The Gangi Grocer's motor sputtered and started up again. As it moved away, the little canoe bucked wildly and the two boys held onto the sides and bounced with the waves. Charlie waited until the water calmed, then he began to paddle toward shore.

"Why did she have to call Dad?" John said. "I'll bet

she stewed about us all the way to town—then all of a sudden she remembered it was Friday." He saw that Charlie was looking puzzled. "Sometimes on Fridays he can leave early for the weekend."

John was worried, but Charlie didn't care. He knew Uncle Paul and Aunt Edie were going to be mad, but still he felt good. He was free for the first time this summer—as free as one of those crazy seagulls. This was more the way he'd thought it would be—he and John out in a boat—sunburned, relaxed. John was a little distracted now, but he'd settle down. And, if he didn't, Charlie would settle without him. "Do you know you can even have a war with kites? What you do is glue broken glass to the kite strings, then each person saws his string against the other guy's until—"

"Are you out of your mind?" John demanded. "My father's going to kill me and all you can talk about is kites!"

"No one's going to kill you," said Charlie, smiling happily as he paddled, liking the feel of the sun on the top of his head.

"You came close. You almost blew me up."

"Sorry about that," Charlie said lazily.

"That one was borderline. A good joke but borderline."

"At least, I finally thought of something."

"Yeah, you did. You thought of a lulu!" John looked at him in sudden consternation. "You wouldn't

102

stop now, would you, Charlie? I mean, you're just getting good at it."

Charlie laughed out loud, feeling real good. "I have stopped," he said. "And so have you. No more joke war. Understand?"

"You sure, Charlie?"

"I'm sure," he said. He knew it might take a while for John to get the message, but he was through. He was going to get on with things. The big parking lot at the point would be perfect for the black bat kite. Enough wind but not too wild. Plenty of room to run with it. And he had to remember to show Rosie the mice in the dining room drawer. Maybe they could make an outside nest and move them when the babies were old enough. They could even go to Beavertail now, if she still wanted to go.

"You dead sure, Charlie?"

"Dead sure!" said Charlie, smiling. "No more joke war."

About the Author

GENE INYART NAMOVICZ graduated from the University of Michigan with a Russian-language degree. She returned to school to get her M.S. in library science from Catholic University. Ms. Namovicz worked as a children's librarian in the Washington, D.C., Public Library for ten years. She helped raise four children and a large variety of pets, including crabs, turtles, and gerbils. Today she lives in Takoma Park, Maryland.